BARU BAY
AUSTRALIA

BOB WEIR AND WENDY WEIR

HYPERION BOOKS FOR CHILDREN
NEW YORK

To the Dreamtime of Our Hearts,
To the Hearts of Our Children,
To the Children of Our Dreams.

First Edition
1 3 5 7 9 10 8 6 4 2
Library of Congress Cataloging-in-Publication Data

Weir, Bob. Baru Bay/Bob Weir and Wendy Weir—1st ed.   p.   cm.
Summary: Tamara explores a beach in Australia and discovers the life-forms that live on and around the coral reef.
ISBN 1-56282-622-0 (book and cassette)
ISBN 1-56282-623-9 (lib. bdg.)
[1. Coral reef animals—Fiction.   2. Zoology—Australia—Fiction.
3. Australia—Fiction.   4. Beaches—Fiction.]   I. Weir, Wendy,
ill.   II. Title. PZ7.W4369Bar 1995 [E]—dc20   93-23325   CIP   AC

The artwork for each picture is prepared using acrylic paints mixed with water on Strathmore Bristol board.
This book is set in 15–point Palatino.

The Walt Disney Company has arranged to have a tree planted for every tree used in the printing of this book.

The Dancing Bear trademark on pages 14 and 19 is used pursuant to the license granted by
Grateful Dead Merchandising, Inc., 1993.

The body paint for Baru Man on page 18 was designed by Galarrwuy Yunupingu. The crocodile is the
totem of his clan, the Gumatj. The sacred diamond pattern represents the crocodile, the fire in the right
hand represents purification, and the eucalyptus leaves in the left hand represent cleansing.

The borders to the illustrations are based upon Aboriginal patterns from the Northern Territory,
Australia. Although traditionally these designs have been painted in the natural earth tones of red
ocher, yellow ocher, white, and black, modern Aboriginal artists have expanded their art to include
a full spectrum of colors.

Special thanks to the following: **Australia:** Tamara Jarvis, Kerrie Jarvis, Mandawuy Yunupingu,
Galarrwuy Yunupingu, Alan James, the children of the Yirrkala Community School,
Dr. Walter Starck, Don and Judy Freeman.
United States: Bill Carter, Tom Paddock, Joseph Englert.

A portion of the proceeds from the sale of *Baru Bay* will be used to benefit the
following nonprofit organizations:
CORAL FOREST
YOTHU YINDI FOUNDATION

For more information about coral reefs and their preservation, contact
Mr. Bill Carter, Director
Coral Forest
400 Montgomery Street, Suite 1040
San Francisco, CA 94104

For more information about the
Aboriginal people of Northern Australia, contact
Mr. Mandawuy Yunupingu, Director
Yothu Yindi Foundation
GPO Box 2727
Darwin, NT 0801
Australia

BARU BAY
AUSTRALIA

The warm salt water splashes lazily against the sailboat as it pulls in to anchor at Baru Bay. Tamara helps her mother and father secure the boat, then walks to the bow and looks around. The bright Australian sun sparkles off the gentle waves. A white sandy beach stretches to a rocky point,

then starts again on the other side. Beyond the point, the color of the water changes from dark blue to light turquoise, showing that a coral reef lies just below the surface. Anchored near the reef is a small fishing boat.

There are still a few hours of daylight left, so Tamara asks her mother, "Can I take the dinghy and go ashore? I promise I'll be back before it gets dark."

"You can go, Tee," her mother says, "but stay away from the mangrove trees at the end of the beach. There might be crocodiles, and I don't want you to get hurt."

"I'll be careful, Mum. I promise!"

She gathers her snorkel, mask, and fins, pulls the orange dinghy to the back of the boat, climbs in, and heads for the beach. A large white pelican looks at her curiously.

Upon reaching the shore, she jumps out and pulls the boat onto the sand. Then she grabs her snorkeling gear and takes off, splashing through the water.

Her approach startles a group of silver gulls, and they fly away, crying loudly at the disruption.

Two beach stone curlews stop looking for food in the shallow water, dash back and forth, then dart swiftly out of her path.

All along the beach there are pretty shells and sand dollars. In some places there are so many that they tinkle like little bells as the waves roll over them.

Tamara bends down to look more closely at a green turban shell. From inside, a tiny hermit crab pokes its head and legs out, then scampers into the water.

9

At the end of the beach she sees a path leading past some mangrove trees into the lush rainforest covering the point. A kookaburra squawks from a nearby bush, and Tamara stops. Is this a warning? Is a crocodile in there? Looking very carefully, she continues on. The cool shade is a welcome relief from the hot sun.

As she walks, the sound of waves fades into the drone of katydids and the chatter of lorikeets. Vines fall and twist from the top of tall eucalyptus and palm trees to the forest floor. High in the branches, large fruit bats hang upside down waiting for dusk, when they will fly out in search of food.

Below, a pair of bright blue butterflies dip down to investigate a black-and-tan goanna before they flutter off into the trees.

Suddenly a loud screeching pierces the air. Tamara looks up and sees a white sulphur-crested cockatoo warning the forest of her approach.

As she watches it, the sound of buzzing reaches her ears. Tamara feels a bite on the back of her neck, then another. Mosquitoes! Turning to swat them, she comes face-to-face with a six-foot carpet python basking in the sun. She screams, shattering the peace of the rainforest. Then she starts to run.

Tamara dashes around the rocky point and down toward the beach, forgetting to pay attention to the mangrove trees at the edge of the water. Hidden among their dense roots is a large old crocodile. He watches her pass. When she reaches the beach, two Aboriginal children and an elderly man run up to her.

"What happened?"
says the young girl.

"Are you okay?" the
boy asks.

14

"Yes, I'm okay," Tamara replies, trying to sound brave. "I saw a huge snake in the forest, and it scared me. That's all." She smiles and adds, "My name is Tamara, but my friends call me Tee. What are your names?"

The elderly man answers. "My daughter's children are learning to speak English in school. He is Baybay, and his sister is Yalmay. We have cooked some of the fish we caught, and we are about to eat. You are welcome to join us."

Tamara hesitates for a moment, then accepts.

As the fish and damper are passed around, the elder turns to Tamara. "Let me tell you a story of our people. It is a story about the land and the water and the life around us.

"At the beginning of time, there was the Dreamtime. Our ancestors rose from the earth in animal and human form. This place was the home of the humpback whale, the stingray, and the crocodile.

"Later, these beings changed. Their spirits became the animals you see today, and their bodies became natural features in the landscape. The whales became these two rugged islands. The stingrays buried themselves in the sand and became the large rocks along this point.

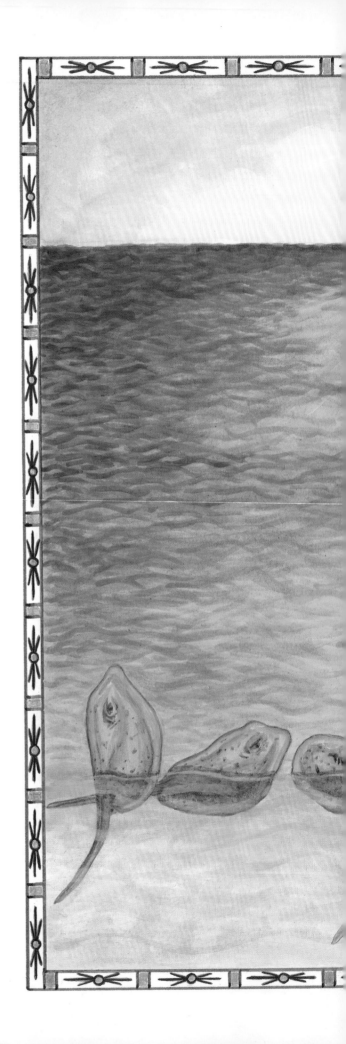

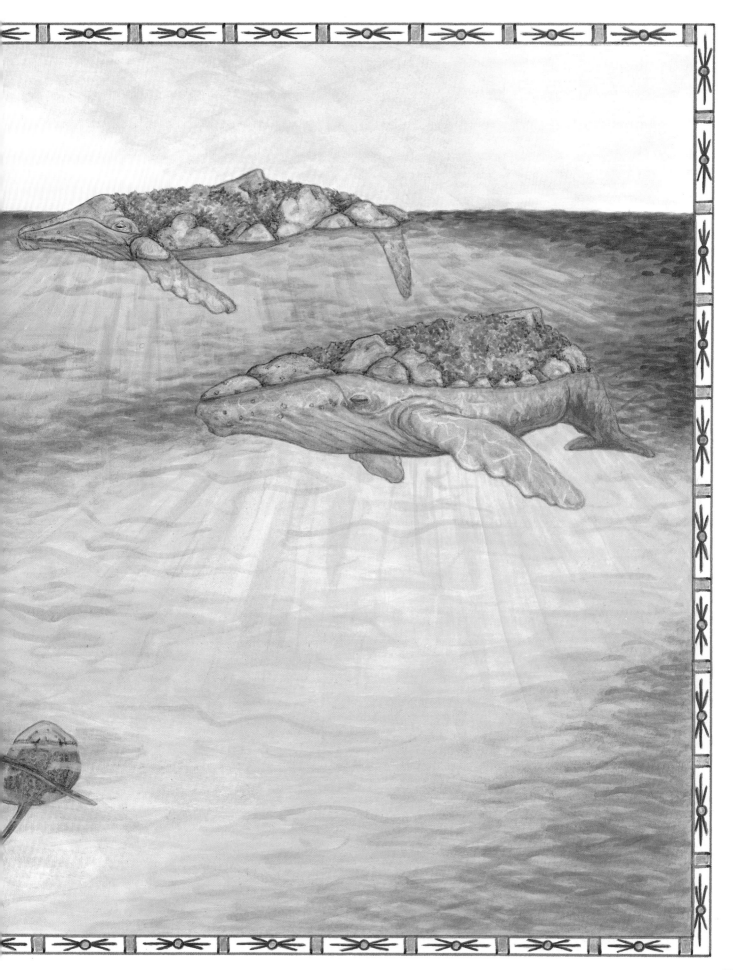

"One of these beings, Baru Man, became a crocodile and brought the gift of fire to our people. He is the totem of our clan. *Baru*, the crocodile, is strong and wise. He will not harm us as long as we all stay together."

After the meal, Baybay looks at Tamara and points to the coral reef. She nods yes, takes off her shirt and cap, grabs her snorkeling gear, and runs with the children into the warm, clear water. They wade out to the reef, being careful not to step on any coral, and gaze down.

Red, yellow, and blue Christmas tree worms decorate a mound of hard coral.

A pair of orange-and-white clown fish hide safely among the stinging arms of a sea anemone.

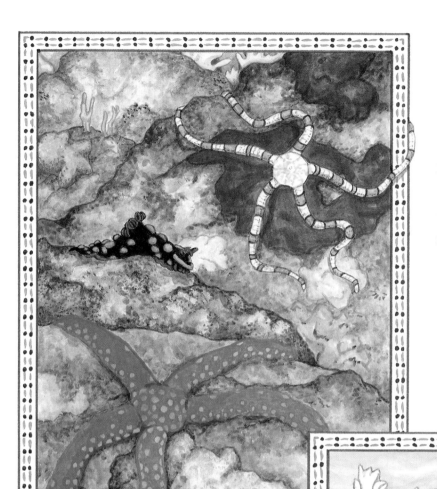

A small neon-colored nudibranch crawls slowly between a brittle star and a brilliant blue sea star.

Above the sea stars, the coral changes from pale blue to bleached white where the water has become too warm for it to live.

As the reef gets deeper, Tamara puts on her snorkeling gear and floats with the gentle current. Beneath her, the multicolored coral in its varied shapes of fans, plates, shrubs, and boulders creates a magical landscape. Tiny clacking shrimp hide among the coral branches. A poisonous olive sea snake glides by a giant clam nestled in the sand.

Two black-and-white moorish idols drift above a moray eel resting in its hole. A parrot fish hangs tail-up as it feeds, scraping algae off the coral with its hard beak. Camouflaged against the reef, a cuttlefish hovers, undisturbed by the harmless white-tip reef shark cruising nearby. Everywhere there is an incredible diversity of forms and color.

Along the outer edge of the reef, Tamara notices that the coral is dead and broken, destroyed by the force of a hurricane. It will take many years for the fragile coral to grow back and for life to return here.

As Tamara follows the reef back towards the beach, the song of a humpback whale far out at sea reaches her ears. Its haunting melody reminds her of the Aboriginal story, and she looks up at the islands.

Instead of the whales, Tamara is surprised by a pair of bottlenose dolphins leaping in front of her. They circle playfully around, clicking to one another, then stop and study her with bright, intelligent eyes. She wants to touch them, but before she can move, they dive gracefully beneath the sea.

Tamara looks down, trying to find them in the darkening water. She hears their clear whistles but cannot see them. Then she notices two large gray forms moving slowly along the bottom. Here they are! she thinks, but it is only a dugong with her young feeding on the sea grass. The dolphins have gone.

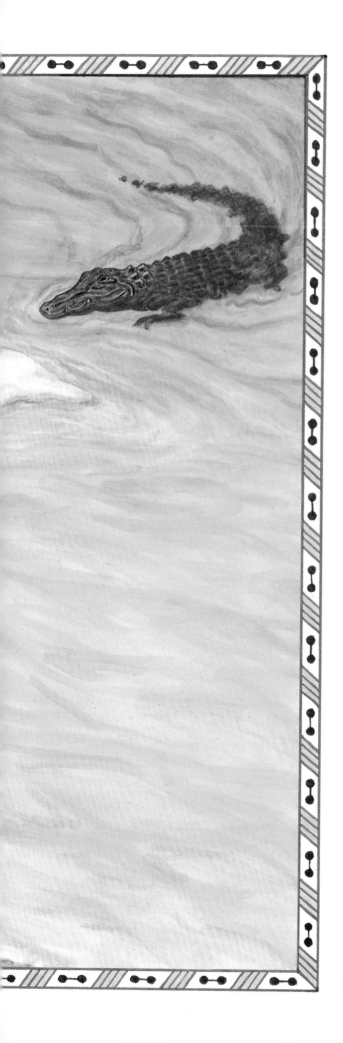

Disappointed, Tamara swims to shore. As she gets out of the water, Yalmay, Baybay, and the elder greet her. She is about to speak when the elder raises his hand and points behind her. "The dolphins are back!" she exclaims, and turns excitedly around. Instead, swimming silently toward them is a huge crocodile.

The elder pulls the children close to him and reminds them, "Don't be afraid. It will not harm us as long as we all stay together."

The crocodile stops on a small sandbar and looks at the people. Slowly its jaws open wide.

Minutes pass.

No one moves.

Then the elder begins to sing a tribal song. Baybay and Yalmay clap to the rhythm. Tamara joins in. The crocodile becomes disturbed by the noise, snaps its jaws shut, and slides into the water. As it swims away, the words of the song trail after it.

Tamara sees that the sun is getting low and it is time to leave. They return to camp, where she gathers her clothes and says good-bye to the family, then walks quickly down the beach. When she reaches the mangroves, she looks carefully around and starts to clap, confident that the Aboriginal song will keep her safe.

As she approaches the dinghy, the sky begins to turn gold. Outlined against the setting sun, the rocks take on the form of stingrays, and the islands become whales. In the distance, two dolphins leap high in the air. Smiling to herself, Tamara pushes the dinghy into the water, starts the engine, and heads for home.

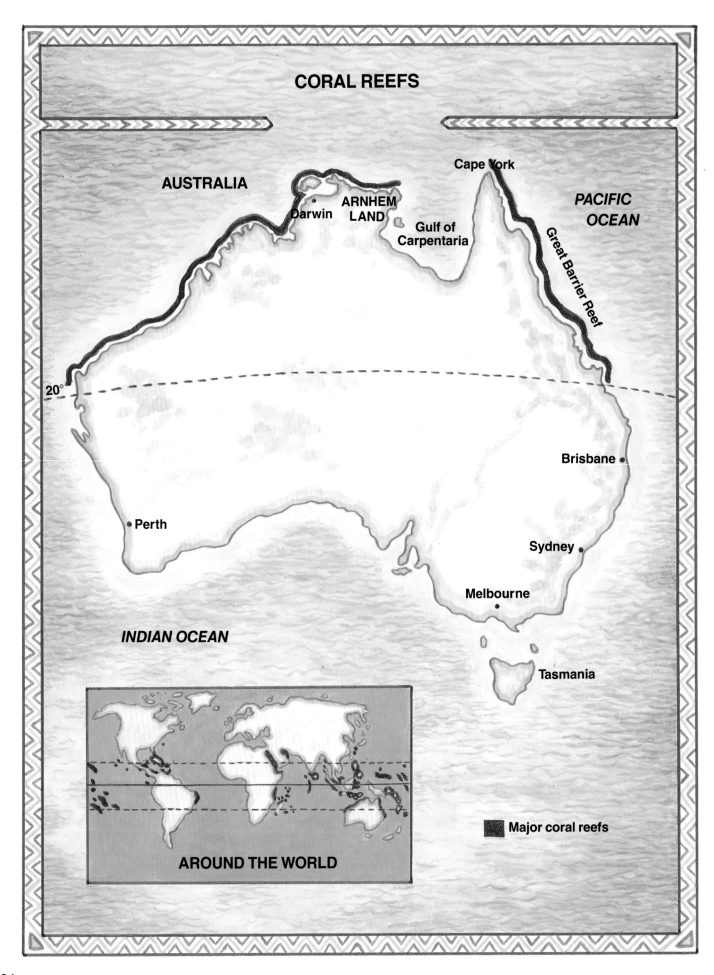

CORAL REEFS

AUSTRALIA

Cape York

PACIFIC OCEAN

Darwin

ARNHEM LAND

Gulf of Carpentaria

Great Barrier Reef

20°

Brisbane

Perth

Sydney

Melbourne

INDIAN OCEAN

Tasmania

Major coral reefs

AROUND THE WORLD

KEY TO THE ILLUSTRATIONS
Animal Names

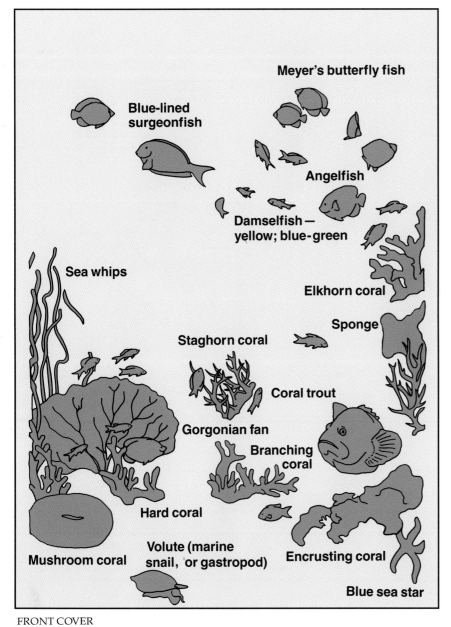

Meyer's butterfly fish

Blue-lined surgeonfish

Angelfish

Damselfish — yellow; blue-green

Sea whips

Elkhorn coral

Sponge

Staghorn coral

Coral trout

Gorgonian fan

Branching coral

Hard coral

Mushroom coral

Volute (marine snail, or gastropod)

Encrusting coral

Blue sea star

FRONT COVER

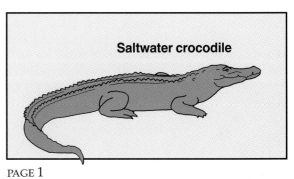

Saltwater crocodile

PAGE 1

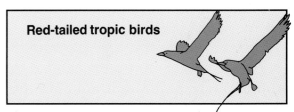

Red-tailed tropic birds

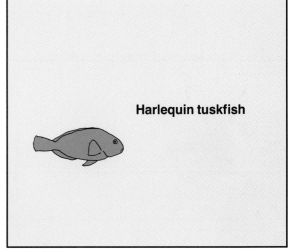

Harlequin tuskfish

PAGE 2

Green turtle

PAGE 3

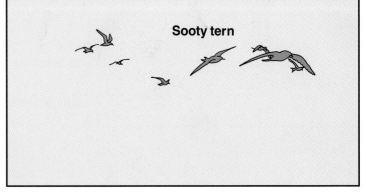

Sooty tern

PAGE 5

35

Australian pelican

Silver gull

PAGE 8

Beach stone curlew

PAGE 7

Hermit crab

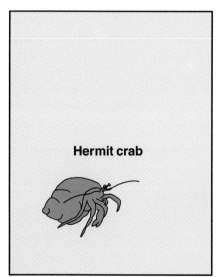

PAGE 9

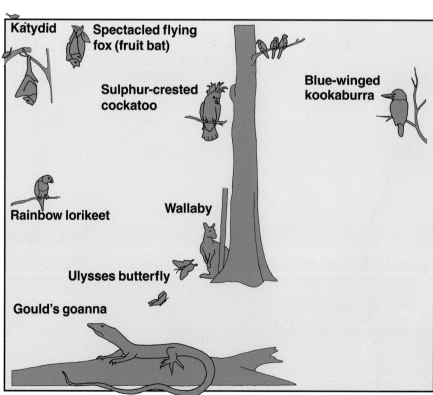

Katydid   Spectacled flying fox (fruit bat)

Sulphur-crested cockatoo

Blue-winged kookaburra

Rainbow lorikeet   Wallaby

Ulysses butterfly

Gould's goanna

PAGES 10 AND 11

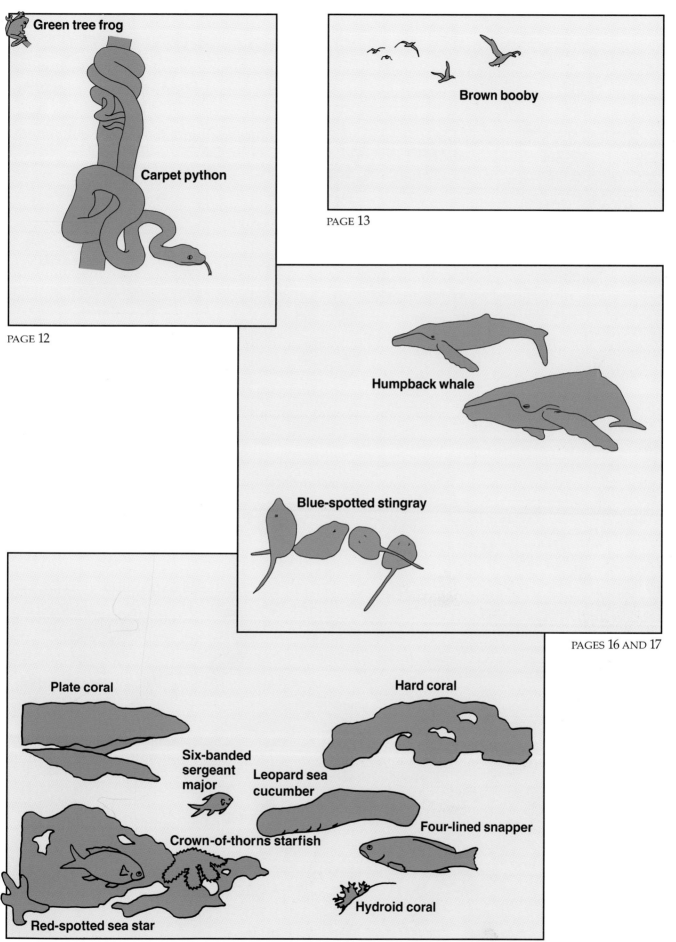

Green tree frog

Carpet python

PAGE 12

Brown booby

PAGE 13

Humpback whale

Blue-spotted stingray

PAGES 16 AND 17

Plate coral

Hard coral

Six-banded sergeant major

Leopard sea cucumber

Four-lined snapper

Crown-of-thorns starfish

Red-spotted sea star

Hydroid coral

PAGE 19

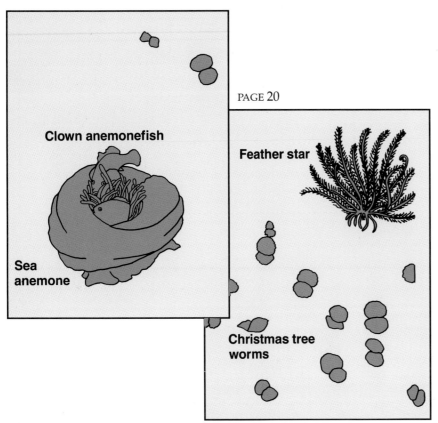

PAGE 20

Clown anemonefish

Sea anemone

Feather star

Christmas tree worms

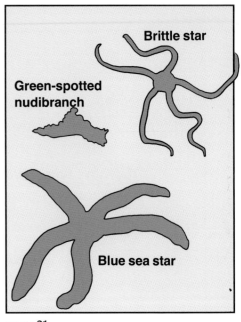

Brittle star

Green-spotted nudibranch

Blue sea star

PAGE 21

PAGES 22 AND 23

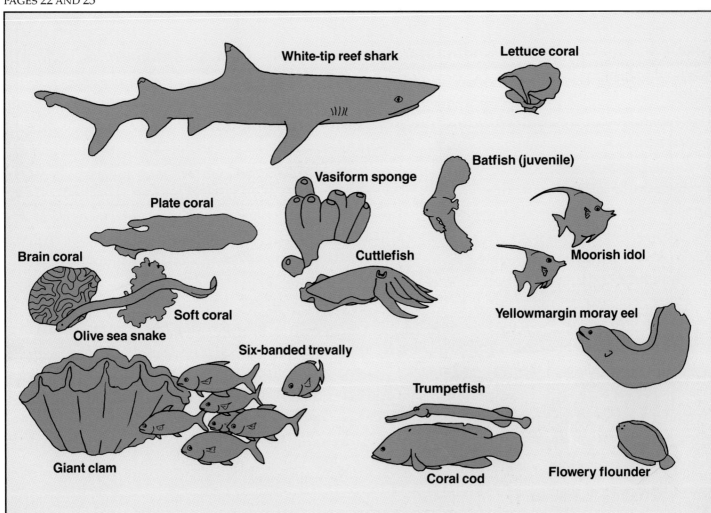

White-tip reef shark

Lettuce coral

Batfish (juvenile)

Vasiform sponge

Plate coral

Moorish idol

Brain coral

Cuttlefish

Soft coral

Yellowmargin moray eel

Olive sea snake

Six-banded trevally

Trumpetfish

Giant clam

Coral cod

Flowery flounder

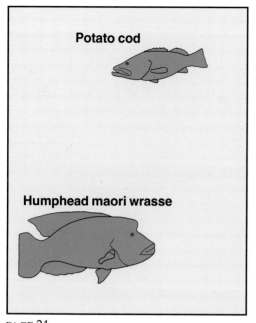

Potato cod

Humphead maori wrasse

PAGE 26

Bottlenose dolphin

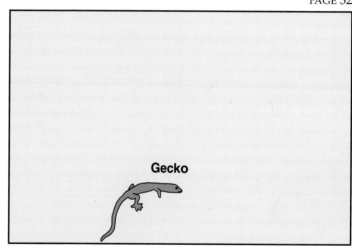

Squirrelfish

Dugong

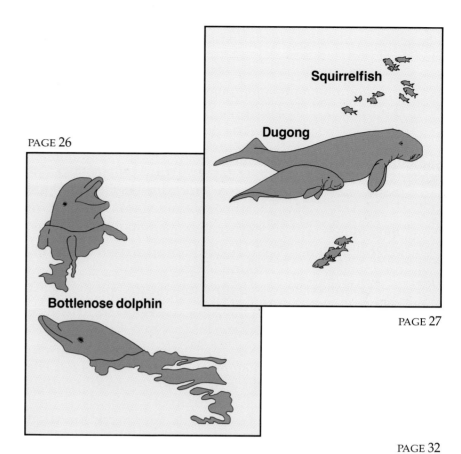

PAGE 32

Butterfly cod

Parrot fish

Soft coral

Sea anemone

Spotted seahorse

Sponge

Emperor angelfish (juvenile)

Banded coral shrimp

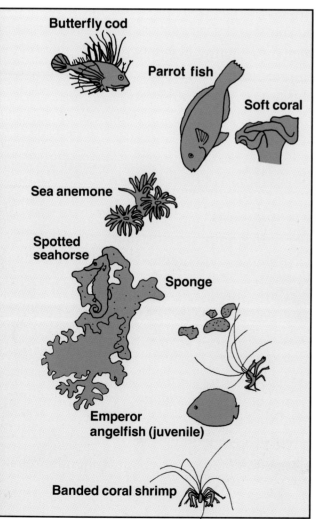

Gecko

BACK COVER

Clown triggerfish

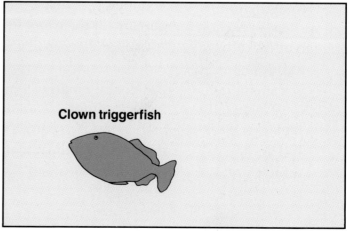

GLOSSARY

Aboriginal The earliest known inhabitant of a country or region. Here it refers to the indigenous people who have lived in Australia for more than fifty thousand years.

Ancestor One from whom a person is descended.

Baru Means "crocodile" in Gumatj, an Aboriginal language from the Cape Arnhem region, Northern Territory, Australia.

Baybay Boy's name meaning "small grove of eucalyptus trees" in Gumatj.

Carpet python A snake about six to twelve feet in length (two to four meters), often found in trees.

Cockatoo A large white-crested parrot.

Coral A limestone base and skeletal deposit formed by numerous living organisms (polyps). Coral dates back 500 million years.

Coral reef A large structure located in warm, tropical waters consisting of many different types of corals. The Great Barrier Reef of Australia is the largest living organism in the world, stretching over 1,200 miles and visible from space. The diversity of life in the coral reefs equals or exceeds that in the rainforest.

Curlew A shorebird.

Cuttlefish A relative of the squid with an internal shell (cuttlebone) that is used to supply cage birds with lime and salt.

Damper A mixture of flour and water cooked inside a fire, like bread.

Dinghy A small boat.

Dreamtime The beginning of time as told in the stories, songs, and dances of the Aboriginal people.

Dugong A slow grass-eating marine mammal; an endangered species.

Eucalyptus A tall Australian evergreen tree with a stringy bark.

Goanna A large monitor lizard with an average length of three feet (one meter).

Katydid A flying green tree insect in tropical rainforests.

Kookaburra An Australian bird of the kingfisher family known for its loud squawking and screeching.

Lorikeet A small, noisy, brilliantly colored parrot.

Mangrove A low tropical tree with stilt roots and fleshy green leaves that grows near the water's edge.

Nudibranch An underwater snail without a shell.

Rainforest A dense tropical evergreen forest.

Sea anemone A sedentary marine animal shaped like a column, with poisonous tentacles around its mouth.

Tamara Girl's name meaning "palm tree" in Russian.

Totem An object or animal that is the symbol of a group of people.

Yalmay Girl's name meaning "beach" in Gumatj.